P9-CSG-500

The Adventures of Zip Velocity

by Bren MacDibble
illustrated by Wayne Bryant

sundance™

Characters

Cody

Mom

Baron von Hairy

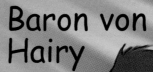

Zip Velocity

2

Contents

Chapter 1

Zip Velocity Rules!

Cody lunged at his mom's ankles as she walked past the table. "Gotcha!"

"Cody, you'll trip me!"

"I'm not Cody. I'm Baron von Hairy, the most evil monkey to ever fly the skies," he said.

"Then get out from under my table, Baron von Hairy," Mom sighed.

"This is my plane, and I'll be in here until that do-gooder hero, Zip Velocity, fights me off," he told her.

"Aha!" said his mom. "Zip Velocity, help me!"

Cody leaped out from under the table, pulled on his flying cap, and yelled, "Don't worry, lady! Zip Velocity will save you." Then he leaped back under the table to grab the imaginary Baron von Hairy. He dove sideways and knocked over a chair.

"Cody," his mom warned, "I'm not going to buy any more Zip Velocity books if you don't stop imitating every crazy stunt he does."

"Zip Velocity isn't crazy. He's the coolest. He's the bravest. He's the smartest. He's . . ."

"He's going to bed because his mom said so." Cody's mom pointed to his room.

Cody stomped off to his room, but he didn't turn the light off. He wanted to read one of his Zip Velocity books.

In this book, the evil monkey, Baron von Hairy, had snuck aboard Zip Velocity's plane. Zip caught him tying parachutes to the cargo and pushing it toward the door.

"Halt, you simian thief!" Cody read out loud.

"Never! The rubies shall be mine," roared Baron von Hairy.

Zip sprang at Baron von Hairy. They landed on a box—and slid out of the doorway into the sky! Zip grabbed onto the wing of the plane and pulled himself up as the evil monkey fell to Earth, still hanging onto the cargo box labeled *Bananas*.

Zip climbed back into the plane and patted the box labeled *Things Hairy Monkeys Hate.*

Cody laughed. "Silly monkey, always thinking of his stomach."

"Turn that light off!" Cody's mother called out.

Cody tucked the book under his bed and lay down.

Chapter 2

Superhero Up Close

Cody was almost asleep when the bed jolted. He sat up and turned on the light. His room was the same. Nobody was there. That's odd, he thought. He turned off the light and lay down again.

This time, the bed shook and jumped off the floor. Cody threw the light back on and sat bolt upright. What was going on?

"Hey, thanks," a voice called out.

There was someone under Cody's bed! Cody leaped off the bed and ran to the door. Just then, Zip Velocity rolled out and stood up.

"Zip Velocity?" Cody asked in amazement.

"That's me. Now, did you see a hairy beast run by?"

"Baron von Hairy?" Cody said.

"You *are* a smart boy. Which way did he go?" Zip Velocity asked.

"I didn't see him," said Cody.

"But I was hot on his trail until I got tangled up under there," said Zip confused.

"But—you're imaginary," Cody said.

Zip pinched Cody hard.

"Ouch!" Cody rubbed his arm.

"Follow me," said Zip as he ran down the hall.

Cody grabbed his book and flying cap and ran after him. He flipped on lights as they ran to the kitchen.

Zip pointed to a bowl of fruit that was now just empty skins. "Aha! We'll get that hairy horror yet."

The back door was open. A banana skin lay in the doorway.

"Watch out for that clever trap," Zip yelled as he hurdled the banana skin.

Cody hurdled after him. "But Baron von Hairy is imaginary too."

"Let's talk about the details after we catch him. Now, he's about your height, very hairy, and wearing . . ."

"A red flying suit!" Cody cut in and held up
the cover of his book.

Zip looked at the picture. "Yes, that's right.
Have you ever thought about being a
sidekick?"

"But you always work alone, Zip," Cody
pointed out.

"Right. But two people would be handy for
this adventure. You take that side of the
backyard, and I'll take this side. Call out if
you see that awful ape," said Zip.

Chapter 3

Little Zipper

"Don't worry, Zip. I'll grab that feral fuzz ball," declared Cody.

Cody ran out into the night, bounded over the seesaw, and headed for his tree house. That's where a monkey would be. Cody was almost up the ladder when a shape flew over his head screaming, "Oook!"

Baron von Hairy landed on top of the swing.

"Zip Velocity, have you shrunk?" the chimp asked.

"Zip, he's here!" Cody called out.

Zip appeared in a flash. "Freeze, you . . . you feral fuzz ball."

"Zip, you didn't tell me you came in two sizes. All this time, I've been battling the whopper version when I could've been picking on someone my own size," von Hairy laughed.

"Come down here and say that," Cody
threatened.

"Look, Little Zipper, I'm not stupid. If I
come down there to fight you, that big lump
of a superhero will grab me," von Hairy said.

"Well, it's a shame you think that," Cody said.
"We were just about to have cake."

"We were?" asked Zip.

"Yes, I'll just get it from the house." Cody ran back into the house and opened the fridge. He grabbed the cake and headed back out.

"Cody, is that you?" his mom yelled from up the hall.

Cody closed the back door quietly. He showed the cake to Zip Velocity. "Would you like a piece?"

Zip bent down and whispered, "Listen little sidekick, this isn't how I tend to go about apprehending the evil monkey. Usually, I just run at him and grab him. Then we run into something dangerous like a speeding train or the sky. It's all very exciting."

"The sky's not dangerous," Cody said.

"It is if you're 6,000 feet up and without a parachute," Zip explained.

"Oh! But this is not the same. This is the real world. Here, if you run into something dangerous, you get hurt," said Cody.

"I'm a superhero. We don't get hurt."

Cody reached out and pinched Zip's arm.

"Ouch!" Zip cried. "What was that awful feeling?"

"Pain," Cody said.

"Well, don't do that again. We have to get out of this weird place. What did you call it? Wheelworld?"

Chapter 4

The Best Book Ever

"The real world," Cody repeated. "I think you came out of this book. It was under my bed." As Cody opened it, the book tingled in his hands.

"Hey, that's me," Zip said, pointing at a picture of himself chasing Baron von Hairy.

"Exactly. We have to get you back in there, but you need to catch the Baron first. Now, go stand at the other end of the seesaw," Cody told him.

Cody laid the book on the ground. He cut a small slice of cake. "Baron von Hairy, would you like some cake?"

"Throw it up here," the chimp called out.

"Oh no, it's much too sticky for that," Cody said. "I'll bring you a slice." He put the rest of the cake on the lower seesaw seat and carried the tiny slice toward the swing and the greedy chimp.

Baron von Hairy's eyes stayed locked on the seesaw seat where most of the cake still sat. He leaped over Cody's head and in one bound he pounced on the bulk of the cake and shoved his fist into it.

"Push down, now!" Cody yelled.

Zip Velocity shoved his end of the seesaw down with all his might.

Up, up, into the air went Baron von Hairy. Up, up, higher went the mangled cake.

Down, down, came Baron von Hairy, heading straight for Cody's book. As he got closer, he became a fine mist and was sucked right back into the book, like water going down a drain.

"How did you do that?" shouted Zip Velocity as he leaped after the monkey.

"I was practicing to be you!" Cody yelled, as Zip turned to mist and was sucked into the book.

"What are you doing?" shouted Cody's mom, running out into the backyard. The cake splattered onto her head. Icing dribbled down her nose.

"That's it! I'm not buying any more Zip Velocity books," she said.

Cody ran and picked up his book. He flipped through the pages. There he was in his flying cap, helping Zip Velocity catch Baron von Hairy.

Cody laughed. "That's ok, I think I already have the best Zip Velocity book ever!"

apprehending
arresting or taking someone into custody

feral
wild; not tame

imitating
copying someone's actions

jolted
shook suddenly

mangled
spoiled; in a mess

parachute
device that allows a person to safely float down through the air from a great height

rubies
dark red gemstones

sidekick
assistant

simian
monkey-like

threatened
suggested harm to another person

Looking at a Narrative

Introduction

(Who? What? Where?)

Who?
Cody
Cody's mom

What?
Cody dreams of being his favorite comic-book hero, Zip Velocity.

Where?
At Cody's house

Problem

(What happens? What goes wrong? How does the character feel?)

When Cody is almost asleep, Zip Velocity appears from under his bed. He is chasing his enemy, Baron von Hairy, but has lost his trail. Cody and Zip find the Baron outside on a swing. They need a plan to capture him.

Resolution
(How the problem is solved)

Cody helps trap the Baron, using a cake to lure him onto the seesaw. Cody and Zip flip the Baron back into the comic book and Zip jumps in after him. Cody is thrilled to have the best Zip Velocity book ever— with him as part of the story.

Adjectives to look for

greedy	do-gooder	whopper	simian	smart
imaginary	big lump	speeding	bolt upright	most evil

Connectives to look for

when	because	But	Just then,	
since	As he got closer,	This time,	All this time,	Then

Author Bren MacDibble

Zip Velocity has captured Baron von Hairy and is flying him back to headquarters when an engine fails.

"Don't worry, my apprehended ape," Zip says. "We have three engines left, but the flight will take an extra hour."

Half an hour later, another engine dies. "Panic not, my seized simian, we still have two engines left, but now the flight will take an extra two hours," Zip declares.

Not long after that, another engine stops working. "Aha, my chained chimp, we can make it on one engine, but now the flight will take an extra three hours," assures Zip.

Baron von Hairy rattles his cage bars and shouts back, "Just don't lose another engine, Zip, or we'll be up here all day!"

Illustrator Wayne Bryant